DREAMWORKS®
MONSTERS
vs
ALIENS™

THE JUNIOR NOVEL

ADAPTED BY
SUSAN KORMAN

HARPER

ENTERTAINMENT
An Imprint of HarperCollinsPublishers

CHAPTER ONE

Beep. *Beep. Beep.*

The technician looked over at the row of computer monitors that lined the wall of the control room.

That's odd, he thought, staring at one of the screens. Things were always very quiet at this secret NASA outpost in Antarctica—so quiet that he and another technician had just been playing paddleball across a cluttered desk.

"Hey, Jerry," he called to the other technician. "You might want to check this one out. It looks like some type of UFO, and it's heading . . ." He watched for a second longer and then looked up again. "This way!"

Jerry gave him a skeptical look. "How many times do I have to tell you, Ben? UFOs don't exist. And we're never going to see—"

Beep. Beep. Beep.

Another computer started beeping rapidly.

"Wow!" Ben exclaimed, watching the path of the object on the screen. "Its energy signature is massive!"

Finally, Jerry came over to look for himself. His eyes grew wide. "What do we do now?" he asked, starting to panic. "No one ever told us what to do if a UFO actually showed up! The whole reason I took this job is because you never have to do anything!"

Ben was frantically typing on a keyboard. "Let me calculate its impact point . . . ," he murmured. He looked up a second later. "It's Modesto, California!" he informed the other technician. "This UFO thing is going to land on Earth, in Modesto, California!"

A dark shadow spilled across Susan Murphy's bed as she slept. Groggily, she opened one eye.

"Agggh!" she screamed. Standing in front of her in the darkness were . . .

My bridesmaids! she realized with a start. What in the world were they doing there, at this time of day?

Before she could say anything, one of the women held up a camera and snapped her picture.

"What are you doing?" Susan cried. "It's five o'clock in the morning!"

"Hurry!" her friend Candy said to the others. "Turn on the TV! Now!"

The screen crackled to life. Standing in front of them, before a map of central California, was weatherman Derek Deitl.

"Today in Modesto, some early morning fog will give way to sunny skies," he announced. "It's a perfect day to stop by the craft show down at the fairgrounds. Or to . . ." A wide smile spread over his face. "Or to marry Susan Murphy."

Susan beamed and let out a contented sigh.

"I love you, baby," Derek added.

"And I love you!" Susan told the TV. Today was her wedding day! It was sure to be the happiest day of her life!

CHAPTER TWO

"You look gorgeous, Susan," her mother said, after the bridesmaids had finished styling the bride's shiny brown hair for the wedding.

"I can't believe it," Mrs. Murphy went on. "My little girl is getting married." She stared at her daughter for a second, a little frown creeping across her face. "I thought we agreed you'd wear your hair up."

"I know, Mom," Susan replied. "But Derek likes it better down."

"Oh, Susan," Mrs. Murphy chided her gently. She snapped her fingers and several bridesmaids instantly descended upon Susan with brushes, curling irons, and bobby pins. Another bridesmaid snapped more pictures of the bride-to-be.

"Mom, please!" Susan exclaimed. "Derek is a broadcast journalist. If there's one thing he knows, it's hair. I'm wearing it down," she added firmly.

When the car pulled up in front of the church a few hours later, Susan's father, Carl, was waiting for her.

"There she is!" he cried eagerly.

"Daddy!" Susan said, hugging him back.

Susan's mother instantly took control. "Hello! Attention, everyone!" she called. "The wedding starts in thirty minutes. Let's get everything ready."

The bridesmaids hopped to their feet while Derek's mother, Rita, hurried over to Susan.

"It's my beautiful daughter-in-law!" she exclaimed.

"Hi, Mama Deitl," Susan said.

Rita grabbed Susan's hands. "Two quick questions: When should we roll out the chocolate fountain, and when will you and Derek be having children?"

"Ummm . . . I . . . I . . . ," Susan stammered. "Can we talk about this later?" she said, backing out of the room and hurrying toward the gazebo outside the church.

She was still standing there, trying to calm herself, when a voice rang out.

"Wow. You look beautiful."

Susan spun around. There was Derek—dashing and handsome in his tuxedo.

"So do you," she answered, smiling at him. "Well, I mean, you look handsome, of course. I . . . Sorry . . . ," she stammered. "I'm a little frazzled. I just spent way too much time with our mothers."

Derek smiled at her. "Don't worry, okay? We'll be alone soon, just the two of us."

"I know." She nodded, and then reached for his hands. "Just think: Soon we'll be sitting by the River Seine in Paris, feeding each other chocolate crepes."

"Um . . . actually . . . ," Derek said uneasily. "I . . ."

Susan looked at him, concerned. "Is something wrong?" she asked.

"No, no! It's just that . . ." Derek hesitated and then blurted out some bad news. "Well, there's been a slight change of plans. We're not going to Paris after all."

"What?" Susan was stunned. "Why not?"

"Because we're going somewhere better," Derek said.

"Better than Paris?" she asked.

"Oh, yeah." Derek nodded.

"Tahiti?" asked Susan.

"Nope. Fresno!" he said.

"Fresno?" Susan echoed, her heart sinking. "In what universe is Fresno, California, better than Paris, Derek?"

"In the 'I've got an audition to become Channel 23's new evening anchor' universe," he responded. "I got a call from the station's general manager, and he wants me to come in immediately. Isn't that great?" he went on.

"Derek, that's . . ." Susan struggled to mask her disappointment. "Amazing!" she forced herself to say. "Fresno is a really big deal, right?"

"We're on our way, babe," he told her. He leaned down and kissed her hand. "Now look, about Paris . . ."

"It's okay," Susan cut him off. "Really. I'm fine with it. As long as we're together, Fresno is the most romantic city in the whole world. I'm so proud of you," she added.

"Of *us*," Derek corrected her. "Not just of me . . . I mean, well, of course, of me. But we're a team now," he went on. "You're proud of *us*."

"Okay." Susan nodded and flashed him a big smile. "Now get out of here. It's bad luck for the groom to see the bride in her wedding dress before the ceremony."

"Oh, come on," Derek told her. "You know I don't believe in that stuff." But a second later he turned around and started toward the church. "I'll be waiting for you at the altar," he called over his shoulder. "The handsome news anchor in the tux. I love you," he added. "There, I said it!"

"I love you, too," Susan called back.

As Derek disappeared inside the church, she stood there for a second longer, replaying their conversation in her mind.

No Paris, she thought, still feeling disappointed. She'd always dreamed of going to

Paris on her honeymoon.

But Derek is going to be a big success, she tried to console herself. *Together we'll . . .*

Just then something flashed in the sky over her head.

It's a meteor—coming straight at me! Susan realized in a panic. She lifted the hem of her gown and started running across the lawn.

But in her high heels and long bridal gown, Susan couldn't move very fast. A second later, the meteor slammed to the ground, knocking Susan over and surrounding her with an ominous green glow.

CHAPTER THREE

"Susan?" cried Mrs. Murphy as she hurried out of the church. She looked toward the gazebo, but there was no sign of her daughter.

"Susan?" her mother called again. "Where could she be?" she muttered under her breath. "Susan? Where are you?"

A second later, Susan appeared in front of her, looking dazed and disheveled.

"There you are!" her mother declared. "Where have you been?" Without waiting for an answer, she grabbed Susan's arm and yanked her toward the church.

Susan shook her head, trying to clear her thoughts. "I think I just got hit by a meteorite," she murmured.

"Oh, Susan," Mrs. Murphy replied. "Every bride feels that way on her wedding day." Her mother suddenly looked at her more closely. "My goodness!" Mrs. Murphy exclaimed. "Oh, honey, you're filthy! Come on, let's get you cleaned up!"

A few minutes later, Susan was ready. Inside the church, the organist began playing the wedding march, and the guests took their places for the ceremony.

As Susan started up the aisle with her father, people in the pews watched, smiling. Derek stood at the altar with the minister, waiting eagerly for her.

When Susan reached them, Derek turned to her and gently lifted the veil concealing her face.

He gasped in surprise. "You're glowing!"

"Thank you," Susan answered sweetly.

"No." Derek shook his head, his eyes wide. "Susan, you're, like, *really* glowing—you're green!"

Susan did still feel woozy from her close call with the meteorite. She reached up to touch her forehead, but noticed that her hand was growing bigger right in front of her eyes. "Oh, no," she said in disbelief.

Susan shot up toward the ceiling and was suddenly very tall.

Derek stared in shock. In the pews, a few guests let out screams.

"Susan?" Derek said in terror.

She was just as frightened. "Derek?" she said, looking around uncertainly. "What's going on? Everyone is shrinking!"

"No!" Derek corrected her. "You're growing!"

"Well, make it stop!" she pleaded.

The minister pulled out his cell phone. "Get me the government!" he cried in a panic.

By now most of the guests were hurrying from the church. Susan's parents had rushed up to the altar.

Susan stood there, shocked. "This is impossible!" At that moment, the garter on her leg snapped and flew off—and knocked out a fleeing guest.

Her mother gasped. "Oh, my goodness! Watch out!"

"This can't be happening," Susan moaned. Just then she shot up another ten feet. She turned to the fleeing crowd. "Wait—wait, everybody, it's okay. Have something to drink while we try to figure this out!" She turned to Derek. "Help me!" She was still growing. "Please do something."

"Duck!" her mother yelled. "Watch the flowers!"

Susan's head burst through the steeple, her arms slamming through several large stained glass windows. Her hair had turned white!

The next thing she knew, military helicopters were hovering above, whirling around her head. On the ground, humvees and soldiers now surrounded the building.

"Oh, Carl!" Mrs. Murphy sobbed to her husband. "Make them stop! It's her wedding day!"

Susan now towered over the roof of the church. She spotted Derek nearby, covered in debris. "Derek! Derek!" she cried. "Are you okay?"

"A beam hit me . . . ," he murmured. "Susan?"

She picked him up in her hand and lifted him into the air. "Thank goodness you're okay," she said. "But what's happening to me?"

Soldiers were throwing grappling hooks onto her.

"All right, don't panic," Derek said. "Don't worry. And whatever you do, don't drop meeeeee—"

The military people had yanked her hard, sending Derek flying. He landed in a parachute held out by a group of Marines.

Susan screamed at the soldiers, who began carting Derek away. "Who are you people? What are you doing? Stop it! Be careful!"

"Get your hands off me!" Derek yelled. "Don't you know who I am?"

Susan frantically tried to free herself to get to him. But the Marines tossed more grappling hooks into her hair.

"Ow!" she cried. "Please leave me alone!"

"Hypodermic team!" yelled one of the soldiers. "Now! Go! Go!"

Several soldiers approached, carrying a massive hypodermic needle. They quickly injected Susan in the leg.

"Noo!" shouted Susan, swatting them away. She yanked the giant syringe out of her leg, but it was too late; she could already feel herself growing drowsy. They must have injected her with a sedative.

"Watch out!" yelled a solider.

Susan swooned and went down. The Marines moved in to secure her with ropes.

"Move it! Move it!" their commander ordered them. "Let's go! Move it! Pull, pull, pull!"

Other soldiers were holding Derek back as he watched in disbelief.

"Derek . . . ," Susan murmured, desperately trying to keep her eyes open. "Please help me . . . ," she pleaded one last time, and then she passed out.

CHAPTER FOUR

Bzzzzz. Bzzzzz.

"Honey?" Susan asked. "Can you hit the snooze button on the alarm clock, please?"

She yawned, stretching, as the alarm continued to buzz. "Derek," she murmured sleepily. "Why did you set the alarm? We're on our honeymoon, silly."

With that, she rolled over and hit the

floor with a thud.

Her eyes flew open. Then she gasped in surprise. She wasn't in a hotel room—she was in some kind of metal cell.

"Hello?" she called out, sitting up. "What's going on?"

The bed where she'd just been sleeping suddenly folded into the wall. Then the doors of the cramped space slammed shut and the room began to drop down rapidly, like an elevator car with severed cables.

Panicked, Susan backed into the wall. As the room continued falling, she could see what looked like the floors of a prison passing by.

At last the cell halted, and with an ominous hiss, the door opened. The next thing she knew, the wall behind her moved forward, forcing her into a large room. It was empty except for a table in the center.

"Hello?" she called out again, looking around nervously.

She walked toward the table.

Crack!

She stepped on a tiny chair, crushing it. As she bent down to pick it up, she heard voices nearby, whispering.

"Is it just legs?" someone asked. "Did they just capture a giant pair of legs?"

"Silence, B.O.B.!" another voice scolded. "She'll hear us!"

Susan turned toward the sound of the voices. They were coming from a hole in the wall.

"How could they hear us?" asked the one named B.O.B. "Legs don't have ears."

"Just shush!" said the other voice.

Susan stepped closer. "Hello?" she said tentatively. "Is someone there? Could you please tell me where I am?"

There was no reply. Instead, a large tube descended from the ceiling, dumping gallons of oatmeal onto the table. Next, a large spoon dropped down.

Susan walked over to the table, which was dripping with oatmeal. Suddenly, something behind her moved.

She spun around. "Hello?"

On the floor was a tall man wearing a white lab coat. His head was that of a cockroach.

"Ewww!" Susan shrieked, swatting at the big-eyed bug-man with the giant spoon.

The cockroach ducked and dodged as Susan tried to smack it. "Hello," he called. "Please stop. I'm Dr. Cockroach, PhD, and . . ."

She slammed the spoon down, just missing him.

"Please be careful!" he cried.

WHAM!

She slammed it again.

"Easy now!" he pleaded.

She stopped, holding the spoon near his head.

"Please," the cockroach went on quickly. "This magnificent brain of mine will be in the Smithsonian Institute one day, so let's not squash it, okay?"

Susan blinked, finally realizing something. "You can talk!" she said in surprise, dropping the spoon. As she backed away from the bug, she slipped on something squishy.

She reached down to pick it up. It was a see-through bluish thing. It jiggled like jelly. Suddenly, an eyeball appeared, and then a mouth.

"Hi, there!" a voice said.

"Aagh!" Susan quickly flicked the slimy thing off her hand.

"Ow! My back!" He laughed. "Just kidding. I don't have a back!"

"Forgive him," said Dr. Cockroach. "As you can see, B.O.B. has no brain."

"It turns out that you don't need one," B.O.B. chimed in. "They're totally overrated. As a matter of fact, I don't even—" Abruptly, he stopped talking. "I forgot how to breathe," he went on in a panic. "I don't know how to breathe. Help me, Dr. Cockroach! Help! Help!"

The cockroach sighed. "B.O.B., suck in," he instructed.

B.O.B. obeyed, taking a deep breath. "Thanks, Doc. You're a lifesaver."

Suddenly, a scaly creature was on top of Susan's head. He looked like a lizard, an ape, and a fish all rolled into one.

He bent down from his perch to peer at her. "Wow, look at you," he said. "I know what you're thinking. It's your first day in prison and you want to take down the toughest guy in the yard. But legally, I've got to warn you, I kind of remember how to do karate."

The creature laughed as he did a back flip, sliding and scurrying down Susan's leg.

"Hi," he introduced himself. "I'm The Missing Link."

Susan's heart was racing. *Where am I?* she

wondered. *What in the world has happened to me?*

The Missing Link looked at Susan. "Gosh, she's speechless."

"*She?*" B.O.B. echoed.

"Yes, B.O.B.," said Dr. Cockroach. "We are in the presence of the rare female monster. Gentlemen," he went on. "I am afraid we are not making a very good first impression on our newcomer."

"At least I'm talking," The Missing Link replied. He sighed. "It's our first new monster in years, and we couldn't get something cool like a wolf man or a mummy."

The cockroach turned to Susan. "Might we ask your name, madame?"

"Susan."

"No, no, no," B.O.B. piped up. "We mean your monster name. Like, what do people scream when they see you coming? 'Look out, here comes . . .'"

He stopped, waiting for her to fill in the blank.

She stared at him, confused. "Susan," she repeated.

"Really?" Dr. Cockroach said, surprised.

Just then, a buzzer went off.

"Oh, yeah!" declared The Missing Link. "It's eat time."

The monsters dove into their seats at the table, waiting for the food to come out. Susan watched in amazement as a pile of fish dropped in front of The Missing Link and Dr. Cockroach got a tasty pile of garbage.

"Oh, good!" he said happily. "An old slipper!"

Then a cannon fired, shooting a ham directly into B.O.B., who just seemed to absorb it.

Susan stood there, stunned. "Please tell me this isn't real," she whispered to herself. "I must have had a nervous breakdown at the wedding, and now I'm in a mental hospital and

I'm on medication and it's giving me halluci-nations."

She backed away, knocking into a big fluffy wall. When she looked up, she spotted a huge furry larvae, more than three hundred feet tall, with antennae. Susan screamed and ran to the other side of the room. The grublike insect shrieked, too.

"Don't scare Insectosaurus!" The Missing Link warned her.

Susan panicked as she looked for a way out. "Every room has a door!" she reasoned. "There's got to be a door here. Where's the door?"

Insectosaurus was freaking out, too. It looked just as scared as Susan did.

"It's okay, buddy," The Missing Link tried to calm him down. "Don't worry about it. Who's a handsome bug?" he went on, rubbing the creature's stomach. "You like it when I rub your tummy, don't you?"

"Please!" Susan cried. "Somebody! I don't belong here. Let me out!" She pounded the walls, which began to shake.

"That is not a good idea!" The Missing Link said in alarm.

But Susan kept it up. "Let me out!" she demanded.

Suddenly a large door swung open and a small man dressed in a military uniform and wearing a jet pack flew into the room.

"Monsters, get back in your cells!" ordered General W. R. Monger.

They turned to obey the order.

Susan heaved a sigh of relief. "Oh, thank goodness. A real person!" She peered at him more closely. "You *are* a real person, right? You're not one of those half-person, half-machine things?"

"Do you mean a cyborg?" asked General Monger.

"Oh, no!" she wailed. "You are a cyborg!"

"Madame, I assure you, I am not a cyborg. The name is General W. R. Monger. I'm in charge of this facility," he explained. "Now, follow me. It is time for your orientation."

She followed him into a cavernous hallway, where several scientists and security personnel looked up from their work to stare at her. Two helicopters hovered like flies around her head as she stepped onto a moving conveyor belt.

The general used his jet pack to buzz around her in the air. "In 1950, it was decided that the public could not handle the truth about monsters. So the government convinced the world that monsters were the stuff of myth and legend, and then locked them away in this here facility."

"But I'm not a monster," Susan protested. "I'm just a regular person. I'm not a danger to anyone or anything." At that moment, she accidentally bumped into one of the helicopters buzzing around her head, and it crashed to the ground.

"Don't let her get me!" yelled the pilot.

"I'm sorry," Susan apologized. "I didn't mean . . ."

Susan watched in dismay as a medivac helicopter whisked away the wounded pilot.

Susan turned to the general as she was conveyed through the enormous prison. "How long will I be here?"

"Indefinitely," he replied.

Her heart sunk. "Can I contact my parents?"

"No," he replied firmly.

"Derek?" she pleaded. "Can I call him?"

"Negative," he answered.

"Do they know where I am?" she asked.

"No, and they never will," General Monger told her. "This place is wrapped in a cover-up and deep-fried in a paranoid conspiracy. There will be zero contact with the outside world."

He paused, and then added, "Except for the first Tuesday of every month, when we bring in the lox and bagels."

"This isn't fair," Susan protested. "I haven't done anything wrong. There was this meteorite, and—"

"Yes, yes," General Monger cut in. "We were tracking it. You absorbed whatever was inside the meteorite."

"So if you know what turned me into a giant, then you can fix me," she pointed out.

"I suppose it's possible," he said, "but I wouldn't count on it."

"Oh . . . ," Susan murmured in dismay. As the conveyor belt moved, she could see the other monsters in their cells: The Missing Link was lifting weights. B.O.B. was pulling off blobs of himself and eating them. Dr. Cockroach was building something that looked like a nuclear reactor.

"Ah, Susan!" he called when he saw her

pass by. "You wouldn't happen to have any uranium on you? I just need a smidge."

The general spoke into his watch. "Take away Dr. Cockroach's toy privileges immediately."

The lift finally stopped outside Susan's cell, and the doors opened.

"We had the prison psychologist redecorate your cell, to try to keep you all calmlike," said the general.

Susan looked into the cell. Above the bed, a poster showed a kitten hanging from a tree.

Susan looked back at the general with tears in her eyes. "But I don't want a poster," she said. "I want a *real* kitten, hanging from a *real* tree. I want to go home."

"Please don't cry," General Monger said. "It makes my knees hurt! Don't think of this as a prison," he went on. "Think of it as a hotel you never leave because it's locked from the outside."

The transporter pushed Susan into her cell.

"Oh, and one other thing," added the general. "The government has changed your name to Ginormica."

Susan slumped in the corner of the cold, gray room, hugging her knees. By now she was supposed to be married, on her way to Paris— or at least Fresno—for her honeymoon.

She swiped helplessly at the giant tears slipping down her cheeks. She'd never felt so hopeless in her entire life.

CHAPTER FIVE

"**B**egin reanimation sequence," a computer voice blared inside a huge alien spacecraft.

A mechanized pod dropped down from the ceiling. Inside the pod, an alien overlord—with an enormous head, four eyes, and long, blue-gray tentacles—woke up.

"Who dares to wake me?" he snarled.

"Quantonium has been located on a distant

planet in the Omega quadrant," answered the computer.

"The Omega quadrant?" repeated Gallaxhar. On a large screen, he watched an image of a planet exploding, and then a meteor tearing through the Milky Way.

"The trajectory of the Quantonium meteor has been traced to Sector 72-4. This planet is known locally as 'Earth,'" the computer told him.

The overlord eyed the picture of Earth. "What a miserable-looking ball of mud. Send robot probe," he commanded.

Several buttons on the central computer lit up as Gallaxhar pressed them. "Extract the Quantonium with extreme prejudice," he said. "I want it all! Every last drop."

"Yes, Gallaxhar," replied the computer.

Gallaxhar cackled softly as a glowing probe broke away from the mother ship and rocketed toward Earth.

"Nothing can stand in my way now," he said softly. "Nothing at all."

It was the middle of the night in Arizona when a bright light flashed in the sky, and then a large, mysterious object crashed to the ground.

At dawn, an armada of military carrier helicopters flew to the site to investigate. News crews immediately covered the area.

"The strange object resembling an enormous robot was first spotted at midnight last night," the TV reporter said into a microphone. "No one knows what it is or where it came from. All branches of the military have been mobilized."

Behind the reporter, a helicopter landed, and viewers could see the president of the United States descending to the ground.

"What's that, Henshaw?" the reporter said, listening to a voice in his earpiece for a second. Then he looked back at the camera.

"Okay, folks, there's breaking news. I have just received word that the president of the United States has arrived at the scene. He will attempt to make first contact with the robot."

The camera followed President Hathaway as he climbed a tall set of steps that had been wheeled up to the large robot. Military helicopters hovered over the president's head while Secret Service crews scanned the ground to make sure he was safe.

The president stepped onto a platform, facing the enormous metallic robot, which was shaped like a bullet with a single gigantic eye. Cameras panned its rusted skin. Its eye seemed to stare intently at the president.

President Hathaway gazed back. Then, to the crowd's surprise, the president flipped a switch on a keyboard, and began to play. For several minutes, he rocked out, as if he were onstage at a concert.

At last the president paused. He threw up

his hands in triumph, waiting to see the alien's reaction.

Slowly, the creature's eye closed. Then it shot out a long metal hand—and smashed the keyboard!

The president raced down the steps, narrowly avoiding being smashed to bits. "Whoa!" he cried. "Commander, do something—and fast!"

"Get in position, boys!" shouted an army commander.

The robot suddenly deployed legs and began to advance.

"Get to your battle stations, soldiers!" shouted the commander.

"You heard the president," shouted Commander Jones. "Light them up!"

Instantly, the army fired a tidal wave of bullets, rockets, and missiles at the robot. A shield appeared to surround it, however, causing the bullets to bounce right off.

"We're getting pummeled down here!" yelled a soldier in panic. "Call in air support!"

Moments later, aircraft began firing missiles at the robot. Once again, the ammunition bounced right off of its force-field. The robot began to walk forward, crushing trees and military equipment as it advanced.

Commander Jones was in a total panic. "Call in a full retreat!" he blurted out.

"Full retreat! Full retreat!" echoed the soldiers. "All troops!"

The Secret Service sprang into action, too, surrounding the president to protect him. "Wheels up!" they cried. "Papa Bear is on the move!"

Within minutes, the president was back inside the White House helicopter, which lifted rapidly toward the sky.

Below, on the ground, the strange alien robot continued moving steadily and destroying everything in its path.

CHAPTER SIX

Inside the War Room, President Hathaway held an emergency meeting with his cabinet and the Joint Chiefs of Staff.

"If that thing walks into a populated area," one advisor declared, "there will be a major catastrophe."

"We need our top scientific minds on this," agreed Military Advisor Hawk.

"This is a disaster," moaned the president.

He turned and placed his hand on a large red button.

"No, sir!" screamed the advisors. "Don't do it, Mr. President. Not yet, sir!"

"That button launches all our nuclear missiles!" Advisor Ortega reminded him.

President Hathaway was annoyed. "Well, then, which button gets me a coffee?" he demanded.

"Uh . . . that would be the other one, sir," someone replied.

President Hathaway scowled as he reached toward another large red button.

"What idiot designed this thing?" he asked.

"You did, sir," answered Advisor Wedgie.

"Fair enough," said the president as his coffee arrived. "Wilson! Fire somebody!"

"Yes, sir," answered Wilson.

"Listen up." The president turned back to his advisors. "I'm not going to go down in history as the president who was in office when the world came to an end. So," he went on, "somebody better think of something to do, and think of it fast." He sipped the coffee and then added, "This is one good cup of joe!"

A door that led onto the balcony suddenly opened with a *swoosh*. General Monger flew into the room on a parachute.

"Mr. President," declared the general. "Not only do I have an idea—I have a plan!"

He landed in front of President Hathaway.

"Conventional weapons have no effect on that thing from space. And we all know that nukes are not an option," the general went on.

"Sure they are," said the president. He leaned forward, ready to push the ALL-OUT NUCLEAR ATTACK button.

His advisors flew into a panic again. "No, sir!" they cried. "Don't do it!"

The president flashed them all a scornful look—but dropped his hand.

45

General Monger put his arm around the president's shoulders. "I'm not going to kid you, Mr. President, these are dark times," he said. "The odds are against us. We need raw power. We need . . . monsters!" he finished.

"Monsters! Of course!" echoed the president. "That's exactly what we need." He lowered his voice. "I'm not following you."

"For the past fifty years, I have captured monsters on the rampage and locked them up in a secret prison facility," General Monger explained. "This facility is so secret, the mere mention of its name is a federal offense!"

Military Advisor Ortega whispered to the advisor next to him. "Is he talking about Area—"

A tranquilizer dart blasted him from out of nowhere before he could finish saying the name of the secret hiding spot.

Everyone in the room turned toward a large screen, where General Monger began projecting pictures of the monsters.

"Mr. President, say hello to Insectosaurus," said the general.

The video showed a close-up of a tiny bug being showered with debris. "Nuclear radiation turned it from a small grub into a three-hundred-and-fifty-foot-tall monster that attacked Tokyo!

"Here we have The Missing Link," the general went on. As the scaly monster's image flashed on the screen, a secretary let out a scream. "He's a twenty-thousand-year-old frozen fish-man who was thawed out by scientists. He escaped—and went on a rampage in his old watering hole."

The next video showed a scientist preparing to film an experiment. General Monger introduced him. "Now this handsome fellow is Dr. Cockroach, PhD. The most brilliant man in the world, he invented a scientific machine that would give humans the cockroach's ability to survive disasters."

On the screen, the scientist entered his machine. A light flashed, and when he stumbled out a few minutes later, the crowd gasped. He had the head of a cockroach!

"Unfortunately, there was a side effect," General Monger stated grimly.

"We call this thing B.O.B.," he went on.

The secretary screamed again.

"Will someone get her out of here?" General Monger snapped. He turned back to the screen. "At a snack food plant, a genetically altered tomato was combined with a chemically altered, ranch-flavored dessert topping. . . ."

On the screen, food scientists were injecting the tomato with the dessert topping. Seconds later, the tomato transformed into a large gooey blue mass.

"The resulting goop gained consciousness," General Monger explained, "becoming an indestructible gelatinous mass."

On the screen, B.O.B. chased the workers from the plant.

"And this is our latest addition to the monster prison," said the general. "Meet Ginormica. . . ."

There was another frightened scream from the table. This time it was the president yelping in terror.

President Hathaway cleared his throat. "General, please continue," he said, trying to sound dignified.

General Monger clicked the remote, displaying more pictures of the enormous monster. "Ginormica's entire body radiates with pure energy, giving her tremendous strength and size. Sir, these monsters are our best, and perhaps only, chance to defeat that robot."

Advisor Wedgie looked skeptical. "Don't we already have an alien problem, General? I don't think we need a monster problem, too."

General Monger narrowed his eyes at Wedgie. "Do you have a better idea, nerd?" Then he approached President Hathaway again. "What do you think, sir?"

The president held up a hand to stop Monger from coming closer. "General," he said forcefully. "I propose we go forward with this 'monsters versus aliens' idea thingy!"

CHAPTER SEVEN

Inside the monster prison, B.O.B. and The Missing Link were playing cards. The Missing Link was about to draw another card. He sneaked a look up at Insectosaurus. The giant bug peeked at B.O.B.'s cards and then signaled The Missing Link by stomping a foot.

The Missing Link nodded discreetly and then reached for a different card. "Gin rummy," he announced a second later. "I win."

"Again?" B.O.B. murmured. "Okay. Well, this time, I shuffle." The Missing Link handed the deck of cards to B.O.B.

Dr. Cockroach hurried over to a radio and snapped off its antenna.

"They called me crazy!" he declared. "But I will show them. I will show them all!" He laughed madly as he dashed back to his experiment.

Wires ran from a large contraption on the floor to another contraption sitting on Susan's head.

She eyed the scientist. "Doctor, please don't do your mad scientist laugh while I'm hooked up to this machine."

The Missing Link looked over at them. "You've been letting that quack experiment on you for weeks," he told Susan.

"I'm not a quack, The Missing Link," Dr. Cockroach said indignantly. "I'm a mad scientist. There is a difference."

"What choice do I have?" Susan said with a sigh. "If he can make me normal size—or even just six foot eight—I can get back to Derek. Throw the switch, Doctor," she told him. "But don't do the laugh."

"Yes, the switch. The switch!" He cackled and then covered up his mouth. "Sorry about that, Susan. I can't help myself!"

Dr. Cockroach threw the switch.

Bolts of pure energy erupted from Susan's body, snaking down the wires—and destroying Dr. Cockroach's machine. The room went black.

"Susan?" Dr. Cockroach called nervously. "Hello?"

Susan felt her eyes flutter open. The monsters stood on her face, gazing down at her with concern.

"Am I small again?" she asked hopefully.

"I'm afraid not, my dear," said Dr. Cockroach. "In fact . . ." He paused. "I think you may have actually grown a couple of feet."

Susan sat up slowly and began peeling off the electrodes attached to her body. "That's okay, Doc. We'll try again tomorrow."

The Missing Link stared at her. "You really don't get it, do you?" he said. "No monster has ever gotten out of here."

"That's not true," B.O.B. put in. "The Invisible Man did."

"No, he didn't," The Missing Link corrected him. "We just told you that so you wouldn't get upset."

"He died of a heart attack twenty-five years ago," Dr. Cockroach added.

"No!" B.O.B. cried, upset.

"Yes." The Missing Link nodded and pointed to a chair. "In that very chair. In fact, he's still there."

B.O.B. looked over at the empty chair, horrified.

"You see what I'm saying?" The Missing Link said to Susan. "Nobody's leaving.

Nobody's ever getting out."

At that moment, General Monger rushed into the room. "Good news, monsters!" he declared. "You're getting out of here!"

"Until today . . . ," The Missing Link muttered under his breath.

A short time later, General Monger led the monsters onto a moving platform.

"So let me get this straight, Monger," said The Missing Link. "You want us to fight an enormous alien robot?"

The general nodded. "And in exchange for saving Earth, the president of the United States has authorized me to grant you your freedom."

The monsters' eyes went wide.

Freedom! Susan thought with a burst of hope.

They were on their way to board a huge transport plane. "I can't believe it," she

murmured. "Soon I'll be back in Derek's arms."
She looked down at her own giant arms. "Or
he'll be in mine," she corrected herself.

The others were thinking about freedom,
too.

"This time tomorrow, I'm going to be eating fresh frogs back in the old lagoon," said
The Missing Link.

"And I'll go back to my lab and finally finish my experiments," B.O.B. chimed in.

"No, B.O.B.," said Dr. Cockroach. "That's
me, remember?"

"Then I'll be a really giant lady," he said.

"That's Susan," Dr. Cockroach reminded
him.

"Fine, then I'll go back to Modesto and be
with Derek," B.O.B. said.

"That's still Susan," The Missing Link told
B.O.B., who was now totally confused.

When they boarded the plane a few minutes later, a soldier called out instructions to

the pilot. "Let's go! Bring her forward! Lift off!"

And with that, the plane took off into the sky. Insectosaurus trailed after it, hypnotized by the bright lights of a helicopter.

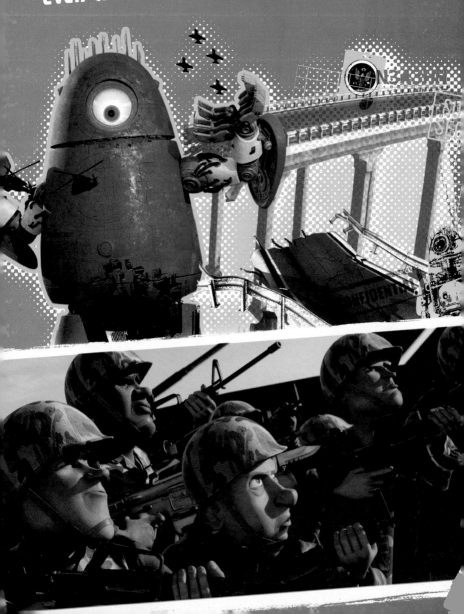
When an alien robot crashes to Earth, not even the U.S. military can stop it.

The government is forced to deploy its deadliest weapon against the robot . . .

a secret stash of fatal fiends!

Watch in awe and horror as a
forty-nine-foot, eleven-inch woman . . .

GINORMICA

a genetically altered tomato
gone horribly wrong . . .

B.O.B. Indestructible GELATINOUS Mass

... battle the enormous robot to save planet Earth!

But wait! There's something MORE sinister lurking . . . an evil alien!

I AM THE ULTIMATE RULER OF THE UNIVERSE GALLAXHAR

CHAPTER EIGHT

Soon, the transport plane from the monster prison landed on a freeway.

Susan drew in a breath as she and the others stepped out of the plane and looked around. Fog surrounded them, but in the distance she could make out a familiar red bridge.

"This is San Francisco!" she realized. "We're not far from my home!"

"Aaah . . . ," Dr. Cockroach sighed happily. "I can feel the wind on my antennae. Isn't it wonderful?"

"I haven't been outside in fifty years," B.O.B. chimed in. "It's amazing out here."

"It's a little hotter than I remember," said The Missing Link with a frown. "Has Earth gotten warmer or something?"

BOOM! BOOM!

Just then, they heard thundering noises.

Footsteps! Susan realized. They came closer and closer, until . . .

A giant, gleaming robot stepped through the fog!

"Hoo-wee!" General Monger let out a low whistle. "Now that's a robot!"

"It's huge," Susan added, suddenly worried about what lay ahead. Was General Monger really expecting them to fight that thing?

General Monger began backing up his truck into the plane. "Try not to damage it too much, monsters," he told them. "I might want to bring it home."

Susan watched in dismay as the doors on the plane slid closed.

Oh, no! she thought. *He's leaving us here!*

"Wait!" she called as the plane lifted into the sky. "What about us? Don't go!"

The robot lumbered toward them. All at once it stopped and shone its giant eye beam at them.

"I think it sees us!" B.O.B. cried in alarm. He tried acting friendly. "Hello! How are you? Welcome. We're here to destroy you!"

Susan stared at the robot in disbelief. "I can't fight that thing! I can't even ... I've never ..." She gasped for breath, terrified.

"Relax," The Missing Link said calmly. "Good old Link has got this thing under control."

"Hide in the city!" Dr. Cockroach urged her. "Go, Susan, you'll be safe there."

She nodded and took off, racing toward downtown San Francisco, while the others stayed behind to fight the robot.

The Missing Link eyed the giant robot. "Finally, some action!" he declared. "I'm going to turn that oversized tin can into a *really dented* oversized tin can!"

Bravely, he marched toward the robot. Suddenly, its arms shot out like weapons. The Missing Link immediately halted and raced back to his friends.

The robot advanced toward them again.

"Wow . . ." B.O.B. murmured. "Would you look at the size of that—"

"Foot!" Dr. Cockroach screamed. "Yikes!"

Dr. Cockroach and The Missing Link dove out of the way as the foot came down nearby, squashing B.O.B.

The robot continued marching with B.O.B. stuck to the bottom of its foot.

"I got him, you guys!" B.O.B. called. "I got

him. Don't worry. I won't let go! I'm wearing him down." He paused while the robot took a thunderous step. "Please tell me he's slowing down."

Dr. Cockroach looked at The Missing Link. "Go ahead," he told him. "I'll meet you in the city."

The Missing Link nodded and hurried away into the bay. Dr. Cockroach swallowed hard as he watched his friend go. Slowly, he turned back to the robot. His eyes widened as he spotted a truck with an old tram in the back.

"Yes!" he cheered to himself. An idea—an amazing, wonderful idea—had just come to him.

CHAPTER NINE

In San Francisco, the National Guard was rapidly evacuating the city.

"Everybody move out in an orderly fashion," a guard boomed into a megaphone. "This is an emergency!"

The alien robot marched closer and closer, the sound of its footsteps echoing all around.

Susan cowered in fear as she heard the robot approaching. She hoped the others were okay.

Boom!

The robot crashed through the buildings nearby. Stepping closer, it focused its huge eye-beam on her!

Susan screamed and ran. She climbed onto a parking garage and raced across rooftops, with the robot close behind her.

As she ran in a panic through the city streets, cars crashed into one another. Watching them, an idea came to her.

Moving fast, she placed each foot into a convertible car and then began roller-skating away.

Meanwhile, The Missing Link was making his way toward the city through its underground sewer system. Finally, he came up through a manhole to look around.

A second later, he spotted Dr. Cockroach coming toward him—driving a turbo-powered, souped-up tram!

"Get in!" Dr. Cockroach called. "I have a plan!"

The Missing Link jumped aboard. Doctor Cockroach laughed maniacally as he hit the controls and the tram shot forward. The Missing Link bounced around inside the car.

They zoomed toward the robot. As the giant beast thundered along, they saw B.O.B., still stuck to the robot's foot.

"Hot dogs!" B.O.B. yelled as the robot passed a vendor's cart. B.O.B. grabbed one, but before he could eat it, the robot's foot came down again, smashing both the blob and the hot dog.

"All right, The Missing Link," explained Dr. Cockroach. "I'm going to pull up alongside the robot. You get up in there, find its central processing unit and—"

"Hey, guys!" B.O.B. had finally spotted them. "Catch me!"

"No, B.O.B.," The Missing Link and Dr. Cockroach said together. "Don't—"

B.O.B. flew off the robot's foot anyway,

landing with a *splat* all over the two of them. Dr. Cockroach frantically tried to peel the goo away from his eyes, but it was too late. He couldn't see to steer—and the trolley car sailed into the water with a loud splash!

Meanwhile, Susan skated onto the Golden Gate Bridge. It was crammed with cars fleeing the city.

"Let's go! Let's go!" a National Guard soldier urged everyone. "Keep it moving! No honking!"

"Excuse me!" Susan called to everyone around her as she zipped along. She could barely control the cars under her feet.

The driver of an oil tank spotted her and panicked, flipping his tanker on top of another car.

"Oh, no!" Susan exclaimed. She immediately circled back to help.

"It's going to be okay," she told the driver,

who was pinned inside the tanker. "Look, I'm going to get you out of there."

Uh-oh, she thought, looking up. The robot was coming through the water toward her again!

"Hold on for a second," she told everyone around her. "We have to get off the bridge before the—"

The robot lunged for Susan. She dodged out of the way in the nick of time.

The heavy robot hit the bridge hard, making it shake violently. Susan backed up as the robot attacked again. This time the huge metallic creature reached out with its powerful claws. It missed Susan but managed to slice several of the bridge's cables.

Suddenly, the panel covering the robot's middle section slid open. Inside, Susan could see vicious-looking grinding equipment with razor-sharp edges.

Desperately, she clung to the side of the

bridge. But as the robot severed more cables, she felt herself, along with huge chunks of the bridge and a line of cars, start to slide toward the grinding mechanism.

"No!" she screamed at the robot. "No! Get away from me!"

Just then, Insectosaurus appeared. Strands of super-strong silk shot out from its nose onto the robot's eyes and temporarily blinded him. The distraction gave Susan time to crawl away. Insectosaurus pulled down on the damaged bridge, straightening it out.

The Missing Link, B.O.B., and Dr. Cockroach wove their way through the cars, desperate to reach Susan.

"Coming through!" B.O.B. said, ignoring the terrified screams of the people around them. "Watch it!"

"Hey, fur ball!" The Missing Link called out to Insectosaurus. "Where have you been?"

The big bug screeched in reply.

"Yeah, I know. It took me a while to reach you," The Missing Link answered. "Papa is a little out of shape."

Susan spun toward the monsters. "That robot is trying to kill me! Why is he doing that? Why would—"

BAM!

With a sudden movement, the robot swung out its huge metallic claw again—and snatched up Susan!

CHAPTER TEN

The monsters stared in horror as the robot gripped Susan tightly. Then, to their amazement, she pried open the robot's claw.

"Wow!" exclaimed The Missing Link, impressed by Susan's strength.

But Susan didn't have time to respond.

The angry robot bashed a hole in the bridge, sending cars plummeting toward the bay below. Behind them, other cars slid forward, about to plunge into the water too.

Susan quickly stuck out one of her massive legs, blocking the cars from falling.

"You're doing great!" B.O.B. told her in awe.

"I'm doing *everything*!" she grunted.

"Not for long," put in The Missing Link. "Come on, you guys, let's take this thing down."

The Missing Link charged the robot. But he was quickly sent flying backward, landing on the hood of a car. He lay there, defeated.

"You hit a deflector shield," Dr. Cockroach explained. He scurried up to Susan's shoulder to take a look at the robot's dangerous grinding equipment. "You can't crush a cockroach!" he said with a cackle. Then he dove inside.

"Ow! Oh!" he murmured as he moved among the sharp equipment. "That hurts!"

Dr. Cockroach carefully inspected all of

the wiring. "Right . . . okay . . ." He crossed two wires, accidentally shocking himself.

The robot's eye lit up as Dr. Cockroach continued experimenting with the wiring.

Susan looked around in a panic. She needed help to save all the people on the bridge.

"Insectosaurus!" she said. But the monster didn't react. It was hypnotized by the bright light of the robot's eye-beam.

Next, she turned to B.O.B. "B.O.B.!"

"What?"

"Help me!" Susan pleaded.

"Sorry," he apologized. "I was staring at a little birdie over there."

"We have to get these people off the bridge," Susan urged him.

"Got it," he replied. He turned and picked up a car, ready to throw it over the edge. The people inside screamed in fright.

"No, B.O.B.!" Susan yelled. "Move the *dividers*—not the people!"

"Oh . . . right . . . ," he murmured. He put down the car and started to eat the concrete dividers.

Susan frantically held off the robot. "Go! Go!" she urged the drivers. Finally the last car drove off the crumbling bridge.

"The Missing Link!" she cried. But he was still out cold. She looked back at B.O.B.

"Ugh . . . ," he said, rubbing his stomach. "I don't feel too good."

I'm on my own here, Susan realized, trying to ignore the knot twisting inside her stomach. *Okay, Susan, you can do this*, she coached herself.

Using the broken cables from the bridge, she pulled up on the robot's arms, yanking it toward her to make it tip. To her astonishment, the robot's weight was no match for her own power.

She watched in disbelief as the robot crashed into the water far below. The rest of the bridge crashed on top of the thing, chopping off its head. Next, Susan scooped up The Missing Link, B.O.B., and Dr. Cockroach, and dove for safety.

The Missing Link suddenly came to. "Look what I did!" he said proudly as he stared at the destroyed robot.

Susan just smiled, and then heaved a deep sigh of relief as the robot's giant eye finally slid closed.

Aboard the alien's mother ship, Gallaxhar stared at a computer monitor, watching the scene as it unfolded on the Golden Gate Bridge.

"Retrieval has failed," the computer announced.

Gallaxhar snarled. "That lower life-form thinks she can steal my Quantonium?"

He slithered down to the floor and barked out an order. "Send another probe at once!"

"Quantonium cannot be retrieved via

robot," the computer voice spoke again. "*Female carbon-based life-form is now too strong.*"

Gallaxhar stared at Susan's face, which filled the computer screen before him. "Oh," he snapped. "I see. You think because you're big and strong, you can destroy my robot probe and send me running and hiding." His voice was filled with anger. "But my days of running and hiding are over."

Just then a tray floated in the air nearby, carrying a teakettle and cup. Gallaxhar calmed himself by pouring out a cup of tea with one of his tentacles.

"Computer, set a course to Earth," he commanded. "I will retrieve the Quantonium myself." He glared at Susan's image. "Even if I need to rip it out from her body, one cell at a time!"

CHAPTER ELEVEN

The huge transport plane carried the monsters back to Modesto, California. Susan sat with her friends, still energized by what had just happened on the Golden Gate Bridge.

"Three weeks ago, if you had asked me to defeat a giant alien robot, I would have said, 'No can do.' But I did it!" she exclaimed. "Me. All by myself!" She turned to the others. "I mean, did you see how strong I was? There probably isn't a jar in this world that I can't open!"

"You were positively heroic, my dear," Dr. Cockroach agreed. "I especially loved how you saved all those people. Nice touch. Wasn't she amazing, The Missing Link?"

"Yeah," The Missing Link said flatly. "She was great. Really cool."

"Oh, poor you," Dr. Cockroach said sympathetically. "After all that tough talk, you were out-monstered by a girl. No wonder you're depressed."

"I'm not depressed," snapped The Missing Link. "I'm tired."

"Why are you tired?" B.O.B. put in. "You didn't do anything."

"I haven't been sleeping well, all right?" The Missing Link shot back. "I've got sleep apnea. It's not fun."

"So Link's a little rusty—I mean sleep deprived," Susan said. "You'll be back to your old self in no time," she told him with a smile. "And so will I."

B.O.B. blinked in surprise. "What happened to the 'there isn't a jar in the world I can't open' stuff? Wait . . . ," he went on. "Did you find a jar you couldn't open? Was it a giant jar? Were there any pickles in it?"

"What my associate is trying to say," Dr. Cockroach cut in, "is that we all think the new Susan is the cat's *me-wow*." He gave a little chuckle at his own joke.

"Thanks, guys," Susan said. "That is so sweet. But I have a normal life waiting for me, you know?"

"Uh . . ." The Missing Link stared at her. "So tell me exactly how this normal life thing works with you being a giant and all."

"I'm not going to be a giant forever," Susan said firmly. "Derek won't rest until we've found a cure for my condition. We're a team."

"I love Derek," B.O.B. said. "You know, I'd

really like to meet him someday."

"I would, too," added Dr. Cockroach. "Dereks are few and far between."

"Really?" Susan replied. "You guys want to meet Derek?"

"I knew it," The Missing Link put in. "We're not normal enough for her. She's ashamed of us."

"No!" Susan protested. "You guys are heroes. You just saved San Francisco. And, more important, you're my friends. Come meet Derek," she added impulsively. "And meet my family, too. They're all super friendly."

"First stop, Modesto!" called out General Monger from the front of the plane. "Ginormica," he said to Susan, "I called your family and let them know you were coming home. I also called the Modesto police department and told them not to shoot at you."

"Thanks, General," Susan replied happily.

It was finally happening—she was going to see Derek and her family again!

When the transport plane landed in Modesto, Susan turned to the monsters. "Okay, now remember, my family and friends aren't used to seeing . . . um . . ." She fumbled for the right words. "Uh, they're not used to seeing anything like . . . well, you. . . . So be cool and follow my lead. Do exactly what I do."

As she whirled toward her parents' house, she accidentally stepped on the fence, completely crushing it. The other monsters instantly began smashing up the rest of it. The Missing Link growled and tore a mailbox out of the ground, hurling it at the windshield of a parked car.

"Stop!" Susan yelled. "I didn't mean for you to follow my lead then—the fence was an accident! Don't destroy anything!"

"Would you make up your mind?" The

Missing Link snapped, annoyed.

Susan's parents had heard all the commotion and come to the front door.

"Susie Q!" Susan's father yelled.

"Mom? Daddy?" Susan's voice cracked with emotion.

Her parents rushed forward to hug her. Now that she was a giant, they only came up to her ankles.

"Did they experiment on you?" asked her mother with concern.

Susan shook her head. "No, Mom, I'm fine."

Mr. and Mrs. Murphy looked past Susan at The Missing Link, B.O.B., and Dr. Cockroach. Fear filled their eyes.

"It's okay," Susan reassured them. "They're with me. These are my new friends."

Dr. Cockroach stepped forward. "It's enchanting to meet you."

B.O.B. shot out to hug Susan's mother. Mrs.

Murphy screamed, but the sound was muffled by B.O.B.'s massive body.

"Oh, Derek," B.O.B. was murmuring. "I missed you so much! Dreaming about how we'd be together again is the only thing that got me through prison. I love you! I love this man!"

"No, B.O.B.," Susan corrected him. "That's my mother, not Derek. And you're suffocating her!"

When B.O.B. finally released Mrs. Murphy, she was so scared, she was shaking uncontrollably.

"Sorry, Mom," Susan apologized. "He's just a hugger."

Susan looked around, suddenly realizing that someone was missing. "Where's Derek?"

"He's at work, sweetie," her mother said gently.

"You know how he is about his career," added her father.

"Well, we're not celebrating without him," Susan declared. "I'm going to go get him!" She whirled around and started walking away from the house.

Mrs. Murphy glanced nervously at the other monsters. "Susan!" she shouted. "What about your"—her voice trembled—"friends?"

"Just put out some chips and dip," Susan called over her shoulder. "I'll be right back!"

CHAPTER TWELVE

fter Susan left to get Derek, everyone stood around awkwardly in the backyard for a few minutes. Finally, The Missing Link put a record on and then walked through the crowd. "How's it going?" he asked as he walked over to the pool. He climbed up on the diving board and called out, "Who wants to go for a swim with the Link?"

No one answered, and he tried to do a complicated dive into the pool . . . only to smash the diving board into splinters!

Meanwhile, B.O.B. had sidled up to the buffet table, where he'd spotted something interesting—a large gelatin mold.

"Hi, I'm Benzoate Ostelyzene Bicarbonate," he introduced himself. "Or you can call me B.O.B. Whichever's easier," he added.

Susan's parents watched nervously.

"Do I come on too strong?" B.O.B. asked the gelatin. I'm sorry. I'm a little rusty. I mean, I've been in prison for my whole life."

"Everyone just stay calm," Mr. Murphy murmured to the guests and his wife. "Whatever you do, don't provoke them."

"Would anyone care for an atomic fizz?" Dr. Cockroach asked, holding up a cup. "It's got quite a—"

BOOM!

The drink exploded.

"—kick," finished Dr. Cockroach.

The Missing Link suddenly burst from the pool, rubbing his eyes frantically. They were bright red. *"Aaaah!"* he screamed. "There's chlorine in my eyes. I can't see!"

He put his arms out in front of him and began walking like a zombie around the backyard.

Mrs. Murphy screamed and ran away, crashing into Insectosaurus, who let out a loud *"SCREECH!"* from above. Susan's mother panicked, racing away from the house.

The monsters froze and looked at each other in confusion. They'd been friendly, and they'd followed Susan's lead. So why in the world were these people so scared of them?

Not far away, Derek worked on his last news broadcast from Modesto.

"That's hilarious, Jim," he was saying to another broadcaster. "It's exactly the kind of down-home humor that I'm going to miss when I'm in Fresno."

He turned back to the camera. "This is Derek Dietl signing off for the very last time. Good night, Modesto!"

"And cut!" called a technician from behind the news set.

Suddenly, the building began to shake. The TV crew screamed in terror. Derek turned toward the window—and spotted a giant eyeball peering through the glass!

"Derek?" said a familiar voice.

Derek gasped. "Susan?"

The door to the stage flew open. Then Susan reached down with her enormous hands and scooped him up.

"Oh, Derek, you wouldn't believe these last three weeks!" she exclaimed. "Thinking about you was the only thing that kept me sane!"

Susan held him so tightly that Derek was gasping for breath.

"Can't . . . breathe . . . ," he managed to say. "Ribs . . . collapsing. . . ."

"Oh, my gosh! Oh, my gosh!" Susan apologized. "I'm so sorry, Derek!" She set him down on the roof of the TV station. "I'm still kind of getting used to my new size and strength," she explained.

"Wow . . ." Derek stared at her in amazement. "You really are big."

"Yes . . . ," Susan said quickly. "I am. But I'm still me! I'm still the same girl you fell in love with."

"Except you did just destroy the Golden Gate Bridge," he reminded her. "It was all over the news."

"Yes, but . . ." Susan tried to explain it to him. "That was the only way I was going to stop that giant robot." She couldn't help smiling a little. "Did you ever think that I could do something like that?"

"No, I didn't," he told her. "I can honestly say

it never, ever, ever, ever, ever occurred to me."

"Look, I know this is a little weird," she went on. "Okay, it's a *lot* weird. But we'll figure it out. Together we can find a way to get me back to normal."

Derek didn't look her in the eye. "Susan, try to look at this from my perspective," he said slowly. "I have an audience that depends on me for news, weather, sports, and heartwarming fluff pieces. Do you really expect me to put all that on hold while you try to undo this thing that happened to *you*? This thing that has absolutely nothing to do with *me*?"

She stared at him with growing dread. "I do," she answered, her voice quaking. "I expected that whatever happens—to either of us—we would face it together. Isn't that what marriage is all about?"

"Technically . . . ," Derek paused for a second, "we're not married. I had it checked out by a lawyer."

"Derek, please. Don't do this," she pleaded.

"You have to face facts, Susan," he said coldly. "And don't crush me for saying this, but things have changed. This will never work out. It's over."

Susan stood there, stunned, as she felt her world crumble.

Derek looked up at her. "Good luck, Susan," he said softly. Then he turned around and walked back into the building.

CHAPTER THIRTEEN

Susan wandered through her home-town, heartbroken.

How could Derek do this to me? she thought. She'd believed that they'd always be together, through good times and bad.

With a sigh, she sat down on top of a gas station. A moment later the monsters hurried up to her.

"Wow," said Dr. Cockroach. "That was

some shindig at your parents' house, Susan! Your parents really know how to throw it down."

"Great party," echoed The Missing Link. "The ladies were all over me."

B.O.B. frowned. "I must have been at a different party, because that's not how I interpreted it all. I don't think your parents like me, and I think that gelatin gave me a fake phone number."

"At least the garbage was free," Dr. Cockroach put in.

"Who are we kidding?" The Missing Link said with a sigh. "We could save every city on the planet and people would still treat us the same way they've always treated us—like monsters."

Susan looked around. "Right. Monsters," she murmured.

"How was Derek?" The Missing Link asked.

Susan shook her head angrily. "Derek is a pompous jerk," she blurted out.

B.O.B. looked up toward the heavens. "Noooooo!" he screamed.

Susan stood up. "Yes," she said firmly. "He said there was an 'us.' There was no 'us.' There was only Derek."

She turned to the others. "What was wrong with me?" she demanded. "The only reason Derek 'cared' about me was because I went along with whatever he wanted."

With a burst of anger, she went over and kicked the gas station building. Dr. Cockroach and The Missing Link jumped off in time, but B.O.B. went flying into the air.

Susan barely noticed. "Why did I even want to get back to normal?" she went on. "The only cool stuff I've ever done happened *after* I became a giant. Fighting an alien robot? That was amazing!"

She knelt in front of her friends. "Meeting

you guys? That was amazing, too. Dr. Cockroach, you can crawl up walls and build a supercomputer out of a pizza box, two cans of hairspray and—"

"A paper clip!" finished Dr. Cockroach.

"Amazing!" Susan turned to The Missing Link. "And you. You hardly need an introduction. You're The Missing Link! You personally carried two hundred and fifty girls off Coco Beach and still had the strength to fight off the National Guard."

"And the Coast Guard, and also the lifeguard!" The Missing Link reminded her.

"Amazing!" Susan echoed.

B.O.B. finally landed nearby.

"B.O.B.!" Susan exclaimed, turning toward him. "Who else could fall from unimaginable heights and end up without a single scratch?"

"The Missing Link?" B.O.B. said, confused.

"You!" Susan told him.

"Wow. That's amazing!" B.O.B. said.

The ground shook as Insectosaurus stomped into view with a *"SCREECH!"*

"Good point, Insectosaurus," said The Missing Link. He turned to Susan. "Don't shortchange yourself, Susan."

"Oh, I'm not going to shortchange myself ever again," Susan declared. "And the name is Ginormica."

"Yes!" The Missing Link cheered her on.

"From now on," Susan continued. "I'm going to—"

Just then, a light beamed down from the sky, striking her. It came from a huge spaceship hovering above them.

"Ginormica!" the others screamed as Susan was drawn up into the ship by a mysterious force.

Insectosaurus frantically shot silk at Susan, pulling her back toward the ground.

"Way to go, Insectosaurus!" The Missing Link called.

From inside the ship, however, someone began firing. Insectosaurus was hit, and Susan was quickly yanked up into the spaceship. As the giant bug went down, The Missing Link rushed over to its side in a panic. "You're going to make it! It's going to be all right," he told his friend. "Look at me. Don't close those eyes. Don't you dare close those eyes! You can't . . ."

But it was too late. Insectosaurus's eyes fluttered closed, and then the creature was still.

CHAPTER FOURTEEN

Groggily, Susan opened her eyes.

What's going on? she thought with a shiver. She was inside a spaceship, dressed in some kind of alien spacesuit. All around her were hundreds of huge robots—just like the one she'd fought in San Francisco.

Slowly, she climbed to her feet.

Zap!

An energy field surrounded her, trapping

her in place. And then an alien appeared out of the shadows, flying on a hover board. The strange creature with four eyes and tentacles said his name was Gallaxhar.

"You must be terrified," he went on, smirking at her. "You wake up in a strange place, wearing strange clothes, imprisoned by a strange being floating on a strange hovering device."

Susan snorted as she faced him. "Hardly," she replied. "It's not the first time!"

"Wow," Gallaxhar retorted. "You must really get around. Take her to the extraction chamber!" he commanded suddenly.

Susan instantly felt the energy field rising, taking her with it. She floated through the air, following Gallaxhar.

"Look," she demanded suddenly. "What is it that you want from me?"

"You have stolen what is rightfully mine!" Gallaxhar snarled.

"I didn't steal anything from you!" she protested.

He whirled toward her. "Your enormous, grotesque body contains Quantonium—the most powerful substance in the universe. Did you really think you could keep it from me?"

"That's what this is about?" Susan demanded. "You destroyed San Francisco. You terrified millions of people. You hurt my friend Insectosaurus. Just to get me?"

"Silence!" Gallaxhar hissed. "Your voice is grating on my ear nubs!" He turned away from her. "It's a shame you won't be around to see what the power of Quantonium can do in the tentacles of someone who knows how to use it."

Susan narrowed her eyes, furious. "I know how to use it just fine!" She punched the force field surrounding her.

"Don't bother. That force field is impenetrable," he told her. "It cannot be destroyed."

That was all Susan needed to hear.

SMASH!

She punched right through it, sending Gallaxhar hurtling backward. Then she tore through the force field, catching the top of it and hurling it at Gallaxhar. He took off with Susan chasing after him.

Suddenly, a door swung closed in front of her.

"Ha!" he snickered. "That should stop your puny—"

She crashed through the door, taking off after him again.

"Computer!" Gallaxhar yelled frantically. "Close hangar door two! Close hangar door three! Hangar door four! Close them all!"

Susan chased after Gallaxhar onto the bridge, where the ship's control room was located. She swiped at him, knocking him off his hover board. He fell but quickly picked himself up.

Susan faced the alien overlord, ready to battle. Abruptly, he turned and ran. As she followed, Gallaxhar pulled down on a lever, which created an extraction chamber all around her.

She swung her arms, trying to smash her way out, while Gallaxhar barked out orders. "Computer, begin extraction!"

Susan punched the chamber walls madly, but it was no use. The extraction process had already started. As the Quantonium left her body, she felt herself growing smaller and smaller—until finally she passed out.

Susan woke a short time later to find Gallaxhar looming over her.

Seeing how tall he was, she realized she had returned to her normal size. Slowly, the extraction chamber opened.

Gallaxhar gloated. "Finally, I can rebuild my civilization on a new planet! Any thoughts on where I should set up my shop? Your planet, perhaps?" he added in a mocking tone.

Desperately, Susan charged at him. "You can't!" she cried. "There are innocent people down there!"

He held her back with an outstretched tentacle. "There were innocent people on *my* home planet before it was destroyed."

"Look," Susan said, realizing that he was too strong for her now. "I'm sorry your planet was destroyed—"

"Don't be," he cut her off. "I'm the one who destroyed it. Computer! Initialize cloning machine!"

A huge apparatus lowered itself from the ceiling and clamped around the alien. Then it lifted with a hiss.

Gallaxhar started speaking. "Many zentons ago, I discovered Quantonium. . . ."

The machine stamped down again.

". . . I was deemed a lunatic and a psycho-path. . . ."

The machine stamped down on the alien once more, but he continued talking. "Then word was passed that the High Senate of Maxilon would find me guilty of high treason. Me!"

Susan watched in shock as the machine continued to stamp down around Gallaxhar. "I vowed from that day on, I would not rest until the Quantonium was mine," the alien finished. Then he stepped into a chamber, and suddenly the ship came to life. Doors opened, spitting out thousands of identical Gallaxhars. Susan watched in horror as the clones marched down the hangar bays and boarded transport ships.

In the middle of it all was a glowing orb.

It's the Quantonium, she realized, an icy shiver traveling up her spine. The powerful substance was fueling the entire alien invasion—and she could do nothing about it.

CHAPTER FIFTEEN

A cross the globe, TV screens flickered with breaking news as people watched in horror.

"Once again, a UFO has landed in America," a reporter announced grimly, "the only country that UFOs ever seem to find." He touched his earpiece as someone spoke to him. "What's that, Henshaw? Okeydoke." He turned back to the camera. "Folks, we now take you live to a transmission from the alien spacecraft."

Pictures flashed from all over the world, showing alien robots landing in such places as Egypt, Paris, and Tokyo. People everywhere stopped to look up as Gallaxhar's face was projected from the spaceship into the sky.

"Humans of Earth," he stated. "I have come in peace. You need not fear me. I mean you no harm."

The humans relaxed a little.

"It is important to note, however," the alien overlord continued, "that most of you will not survive the next twenty-four hours. Those of you who do survive will be enslaved and experimented on." Gallaxhar gave a shrug. "You should in no way take this personally. It's just business."

People watching from the ground stared at him in horror. Many were already running away, desperately looking for places to hide.

"To recap," the alien commander said, his

eyes gleaming with malice. "I come in peace. I mean you no harm. And you will all die. Gallaxhar, out," he finished.

Far below Gallaxhar's ship, the monsters stood near Insectosaurus's lifeless body, their hearts broken.

"What are we going to do now, Doc?" B.O.B. murmured.

"I . . . ," Doctor Cockroach faltered. "I don't know," he confessed.

"You don't know?" B.O.B. echoed in disbelief. "But you never don't know, Doc."

Dr. Cockroach nodded. "I know."

"I'll tell you what we're going to do," The Missing Link said grimly. "We're not going to let Insectosaurus die in vain." He looked up toward the sky. "We're going up there to find Susan, and then we're going to take that alien down!"

* * *

Hours later, the monsters were on board the military transport plane again, soaring toward Gallaxhar's spaceship.

General Monger had equipped them all with jet packs. Now he paced before them, outlining the plan.

"All right, gentlemen," he boomed. "You've got enough juice in those jet packs to get up there. But you don't have enough to make it home. I'll come to get you if I can. But if I don't, it means I'm dead. Or late," he added. "So wait for me for as long as you can."

He took a step back and saluted them sharply.

"That's rude!" B.O.B. declared. "What did we do?"

"No, B.O.B.," Dr. Cockroach explained patiently. "Saluting someone is not rude. It's a sign of respect."

As the plane approached the alien space-ship, the cargo doors slid open. The monsters activated their jet packs and stepped through the doorway into the sky.

The pilot stared through the windshield in the cockpit. A laser beam from the spaceship was aimed in their direction!

"General!" he called out. "The ship . . . it's targeting us!"

"Hold your course, Lieutenant!" ordered the general.

The aliens fired.

"Hard right!" the general screamed at the pilot. "Hard right!"

The pilot tried desperately to dodge the laser. "I can't shake it!" he yelled.

BOOM!

The plane exploded as the laser found its target. General Monger scooped up the pilot and quickly activated his parachute. He sailed back down to Earth and landed safely—right on top of Insectosaurus, who still lay lifelessly near the gas station.

"That's why I always wear a parachute, Lieutenant!" General Monger declared.

Suddenly, there was a strange sound at their feet.

"Insectosaurus . . . ?" the general said in surprise.

CHAPTER SIXTEEN

The monsters slipped aboard Gallax-har's ship. As they stood, trying to get their bearings, B.O.B. oozed out from behind a robot.

"Kree-kraw, kree-kraw!" he squeaked.

Dr. Cockroach frowned at him. "Who are you signaling, B.O.B.? We're right here!"

"Shhh!" The Missing Link scolded them, afraid someone would hear.

All around, they saw the trail of debris left by Susan as she had raced through the ship after Gallaxhar. The monsters quickly shed their jet packs and followed the trail.

The monsters watched from a tunnel as a hologram of Gallaxhar gave orders to a clone who was holding on to Susan.

"Gallaxhar," he ordered the clone. "Take the prisoner to the incinerator! She's useless to us now."

"Hail, Gallaxhar!" said the clone as he led her away.

"Wow . . . ," The Missing Link murmured. "Ginormica isn't so giant anymore."

"How are we supposed to get to her?" Dr. Cockroach asked in dismay. He glanced at the globe of Quantonium that was still spitting out hundreds of clones. "There are too many of them!"

B.O.B. watched for a second. Then he blurted out, "I may not have a brain, gentlemen.

But I do have an idea!"

They rummaged through a storage closet for disguises, and minutes later the monsters put B.O.B.'s plan into action.

As the clone passed, pulling Susan along, The Missing Link jumped out in front of him. The three monsters were all dressed in Gallaxhar's uniform.

"Halt!" The Missing Link commanded.

Susan looked up, relief washing over her. Her friends had come for her!

"I, Gallaxhar, command you to hand over the prisoner this instant!" The Missing Link ordered the clone.

"Clearly, you are defective beyond repair!" the clone replied. "Guards! Take this defective clone to the incinerator!"

Susan held her breath. But no one came forward to grab The Missing Link.

"Well, what are you waiting for?" demanded the clone. "You! And you!" He pointed to Dr.

Cockroach and B.O.B.

Dr. Cockroach looked at him in surprise. "Seriously?"

"Yes!" the clone responded. "Take the prisoner and the defective clone to the incinerator now!"

"Uhhh . . . ," Dr. Cockroach sputtered. "Of course, Gallaxhar, sir!"

"And here's a security pass, just in case," added the clone. "Would you like a weapon, too?"

"Yes, I would!" said B.O.B. as the clone handed it over. Then B.O.B. whispered to his friends, "Hey, guys! Look!"

"You know where the incinerator is, of course?" asked the clone.

The monsters stared at him blankly.

The clone shook his head and sighed. "Go all the way down this hallway. Take your first left, your third right, and a quick left. Don't go right—that will lead you right off the ship.

And then, take the elevator down to the incinerator level. Be quick about it!"

With that, he left them.

Susan and the monsters marched off, following the clone's directions to the exit, not the incinerator.

"I can't believe you came to save me," Susan said gratefully. "I don't know what to say!"

"You don't have to say anything," Dr. Cockroach said. "After all, my dear—" Just then, he spotted some clones coming around the corner. "—you're nothing but a filthy carbon-based lifeform! We should take her to the incinerator!"

"Hail, Gallaxhar!" shouted the clones as they marched past.

"Man, these disguises are rad," said B.O.B.

Dr. Cockroach pushed Susan toward the exit. "All right, time for you to go, my dear."

"Shouldn't Ginormica be helping us?" asked B.O.B.

"I wish I could, but I'm not Ginormica anymore," Susan pointed out.

The monsters turned to leave. Suddenly, B.O.B. hurried back to Susan.

"I once read something very profound," he told her. "And let me tell you, it changed the way I look at the world."

She smiled, waiting for him to finish.

"It said, 'Objects in the mirror may be larger than they appear.'"

B.O.B. turned her head so she could see herself in the shiny elevator door, before running off. She stared at her reflection. She was normal-sized now, but nothing would ever be the same again. Susan closed her eyes, trying not to think about what lay ahead, for her and for her friends.

Then the elevator door opened, and she was face-to-face with a group of clones! Susan took off running back through the ship.

* * *

The monsters walked through the ship in their disguises, whispering to each other. Whenever they passed clones, they would cry out "Hail, Gallaxhar!"

"The only way to save Earth," said Dr. Cockroach, "is to blow up this ship before the invasion starts. It won't be easy. We need to find the main power core."

B.O.B. oozed up to the next clone they saw. "Excuse me," he asked, "Could you point us in the direction of the main power core?"

"It's right there, above the extraction chamber," said the clone, pointing.

"Thank you! Hail, Gallaxhar," said B.O.B.

"All right," said The Missing Link, "let's do this!" He ripped off his uniform, and suddenly all the clones turned to him.

"Monsters!" the clones cried.

"Aliens!" shouted The Missing Link, B.O.B., and Dr. Cockroach at the same time, springing into action.

The Missing Link fought his way through the clones and tossed Dr. Cockroach up on top of the central computer.

"Go, Doc! We'll hold them off!"

The scientist slipped inside and gazed around, impressed by the alien technology. The computer sounded a warning.

"Warning! Intruder."

The Missing Link charged at the clones, grabbing the bottom of a hover board and hoisting himself up to face its passenger. "How's it going?" he said before tossing the clone overboard. He swung around like an ape, smashing into more hover boards and taking out clones, one by one. He thumped his chest proudly.

B.O.B. engulfed one clone and then another. He popped them out over the bridge for a long fall.

Dr. Cockroach laughed madly as he rewired the circuits, and now lights were flashing everywhere.

"*Ship has sustained internal damage. Invasion no longer possible*," announced the computer voice.

On the main deck, Gallaxhar heard the warning and shouted orders. "Close off all the blast doors! Seal the middle of the ship!"

As doors began to slam shut around the monsters, The Missing Link yanked Dr. Cockroach and B.O.B. up onto his hover board.

He shot toward the door just as Susan raced toward them.

"Susan!" The Missing Link yelled. She had been running all over the ship as the army of clones from the elevator chased her. Now one of the clones was closing in on her. His hover board got stuck in the closing doors, which sent the clone flying. Susan had ducked, and now she called to her friends to hurry out the door.

"Hurry up, you guys! You can make it!" she shouted.

But before they could reach her, the heavy door slammed shut, trapping the monsters inside.

CHAPTER SEVENTEEN

S usan stood there for a second, frozen. Suddenly, a voice rang out. It was Gallaxhar speaking from the bridge.

"Computer, divert Quantonium to the bridge!"

The Quantonium began flowing from the cloning machine to the main deck, where a giant statue of Gallaxhar held aloft a ball that slowly filled with the glowing energy.

The Missing Link tried to punch through the door. "It's no use," he said finally. "I can't get through!"

"Hang tight!" Susan shouted to her friends. "I'll get you out of there! I'm not leaving without you!"

Susan eyed some hover boards floating nearby in the air. She placed a foot on each one and took off, using them as roller skates.

"Okay, Susan, you can do this," she told herself firmly.

"Female carbon-based life-form not contained," announced the computer voice.

"Activate robot probes! Crush her!" Gallaxhar commanded.

Giant robots, just like the ones that had landed on Earth, came to life around Susan. Their mechanical arms started reaching for her. Susan used the hover boards to fly around them, confusing the robots and causing them to crash into each other. Then she sailed out of the spaceship and into the sky.

Abruptly, she turned around and headed back toward the ship. Gallaxhar glared in fury and fired a photon cannon.

Susan sailed nimbly around it. She turned toward the bridge, breaking off one piece of her hover board and flinging it at a glass wall, shattering it.

Gallaxhar lifted his laser gun toward her, but he was blown back by the shattered glass. The gun slid across the floor as Susan entered the bridge, ready to confront him.

"It's over, Gallaxhar," she said. "Now open the doors and let my friends go."

The computer voice spoke again: "Quantonium ready for absorption."

Gallaxhar scrambled to his feet and raced toward the glowing orb, where the Quantonium was pooling.

Susan reacted quickly. As Gallaxhar tried to scramble up, she grabbed two of his tentacles and yanked hard.

Gallaxhar fell to the ground. He wrapped his other tentacles around her waist and pulled her hard to the floor. As they wrestled for a few minutes, Susan spotted the laser gun lying on the floor. She tried to reach for it, but it was too far away.

She wriggled around to face Gallaxhar again, yanking hard on his antennae.

"Ah!" he screamed, letting go of his hold on her. "My zaznoids!"

She reached out and scooped up the weapon. Then she aimed the laser at him.

"It's over, Gallaxhar," Susan declared.

He raised his hands and tentacles in the air, surrendering.

Just then the ship began shaking violently.

"Reactor core meltdown," blared the computer voice. *"Total annihilation in T minus two minutes."*

Susan's heart skipped a beat. *Total annihi-*

lation, she thought in a panic. Dr. Cockroach, The Missing Link, and B.O.B. were still trapped inside the ship!

The monsters began banging hard on the heavy blast doors.

Gallaxhar looked around anxiously. "I think it's time we cut ourselves a little deal," he said to Susan. "I'll open the doors if you split the Quantonium with me. What do you say, sixty-forty?"

Susan stared at him. "I know another way," she said. Gallaxhar braced himself, ready for her to shoot.

Instead, Susan lifted the gun and fired upward, shearing off the arms of the statue that held the glowing orb. Gallaxhar leaped up as the orb landed directly on Susan. But one of the statue's tentacles fell on him, trapping him underneath it.

All around the monsters, the ship was exploding and crumbling.

"*Total annihilation in T minus one minute,*" said the computer.

"It's been an honor knowing you, Doc," murmured The Missing Link.

"The feeling's mutual, my friend," responded Dr. Cockroach.

More debris crashed nearby.

"I'll see you both tomorrow," said B.O.B.

Dr. Cockroach gave a sad smile, not wanting to tell B.O.B. the truth. "That's right, B.O.B. . . . and there will be candy, cake, and balloons."

BOOM!

From above, there was a loud crash, and then Susan punched her way through the ceiling. She landed in front of them, catching a piece of the ship just before it crushed them.

"Hogan's goat!" cried Dr. Cockroach. "It's Susan!"

"Correction, Doc," said The Missing Link, grinning. "It's Ginormica!"

The computer spoke again. *"Total annihilation in T minus thirty seconds."*

The platform beneath their feet exploded. Susan grabbed the monsters, and they all tumbled down toward the bottom of the ship. She punched her way through the hull and then managed to pull them over to a ledge.

"Where's General Monger?" Susan demanded, as the computer announced that there were fifteen seconds left.

The Missing Link looked around frantically. "He's supposed to be here!"

"He said the only reason he wouldn't be here is if he were dead," Dr. Cockroach reminded them.

The computer began counting down. *"Ten... nine..."*

Then, to their astonishment, General Monger suddenly appeared, riding Insectosaurus. The monster had transformed into a giant butterfly!

The Missing Link stared at Insectosaurus in

disbelief. "You're alive!" he declared happily.

"*Six . . . five . . . four . . .* ," the computer counted down.

"Come on!" cried General Monger.

Susan and the monsters scrambled onto Insectosaurus's back and flew off—just in the nick of time.

Inside the bridge, Gallaxhar had managed to wriggle out from underneath the statue's heavy tentacle. An escape pod jettisoned toward him.

"*One!*" announced the computer.

The monster ship exploded, shattering into a million tiny pieces in the sky.

CHAPTER EIGHTEEN

ews reporters and camera crews were camped out all over the White House lawn.

"Breaking news," a broadcaster said into a TV camera. "A ceremony honoring the monsters who saved Earth is taking place at the White House."

The monsters approached President Hathaway, who waved at the cheering crowd of thousands. In the sky above, Butterflyosaurus joined the Air Force in a dramatic flyby for the crowd.

The president addressed the monsters. "Job well done," he told them. "Earth has been saved, and we owe it all to you. In appreciation of your efforts, we would like to return you to a maximum security prison of your choice."

The monsters looked shocked.

One of the president's advisors leaned over and whispered something to him.

"What's that?" President Hathaway said in confusion. "Oh, right, that's an old speech. Sorry."

He pulled a new sheet of paper from his pocket and quickly reviewed it.

"On behalf of the world," the president said, "I would like to present you with the Presidential Beads of Gratitude!"

The crowd cheered and the monsters beamed happily as necklaces were placed around their necks. They'd done it! They'd saved Earth from an alien invasion!

Susan's parents walked up to The Missing Link.

"Link, I'm sorry we all ran away screaming the last time we saw you," said Carl Murphy. "Come back and we'll throw you a real party."

Dr. Cockroach walked over to Ginormica. The Missing Link and B.O.B. joined him.

"Susan, we never thanked you for saving our lives."

"You don't need to thank me," she said.

There was a loud *"SCREEECH!"* from above.

"Butterflyosaurus is right. You gave up being normal to save us," said The Missing Link.

Susan gave her big shoulders a shrug. "Let's face it," she said with a smile. "Being normal is overrated."

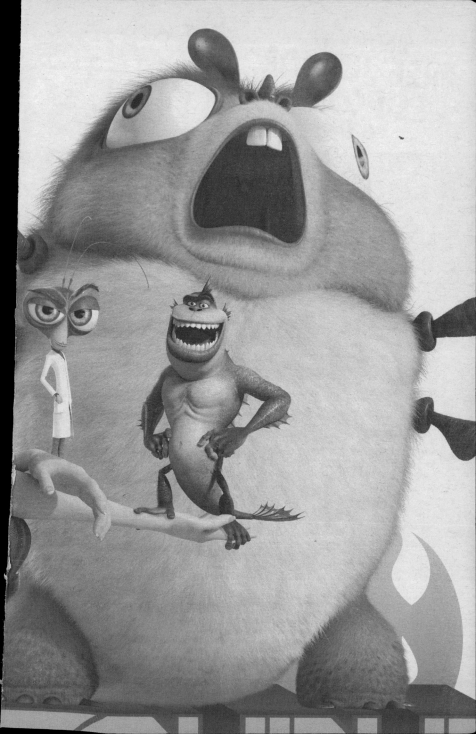

ENJOY A FREE JUNIOR POPCORN WHEN YOU SEE

DREAMWORKS
MONSTERS vs ALIENS

INTRU3D

Monsters vs. Aliens © 2008 DreamWorks Animation L.L.C. All Rights Reserved.

PLEASE BRING IN THIS BOOK PAGE TO ANY PARTICIPATING CINEMARK THEATRE PLAYING MONSTERS VS. ALIENS TO RECEIVE ONE FREE JUNIOR POPCORN!

Offer good Monday through Thursday.

courtesy of

CINEMARK ®

CENTURY THEATRES. CinéArts Tinseltown

Visit the official MONSTERS VS. ALIENS website @ www.monstersvsaliens.com
INVADING THEATRES ON MARCH 27, 2009!